NOV 2023

Construction Site:
Taking Flight!

SHERRI DUSKEY RINKER AND AG FORD

Construction Site:
Taking Flight!

chronicle books·san francisco

Six truck friends are on their way
to start a brand-new job today.

They're off to work
and feeling strong!

But . . . traffic's *slooow*. The lines are long.
They can barely roll at all. . . .

This whole airport is way too small!
Everyone must sit and wait—

on streets, on runways, at the gate.
And *everyone* is running late!

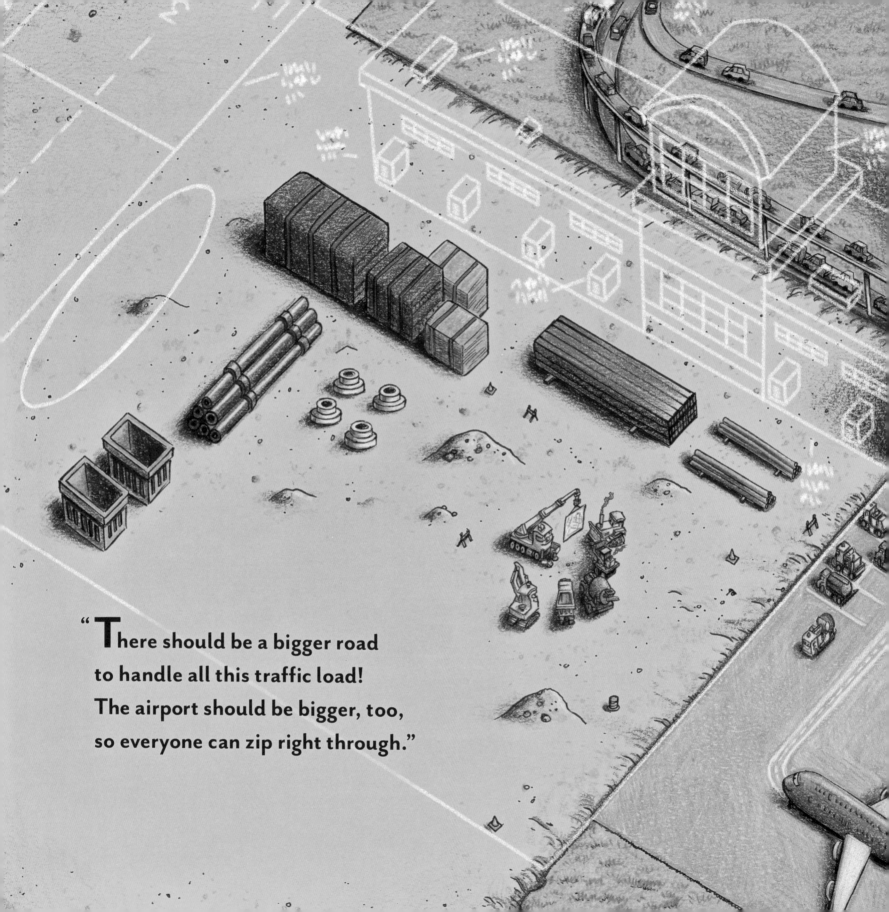

"There should be a bigger road
to handle all this traffic load!
The airport should be bigger, too,
so everyone can zip right through."

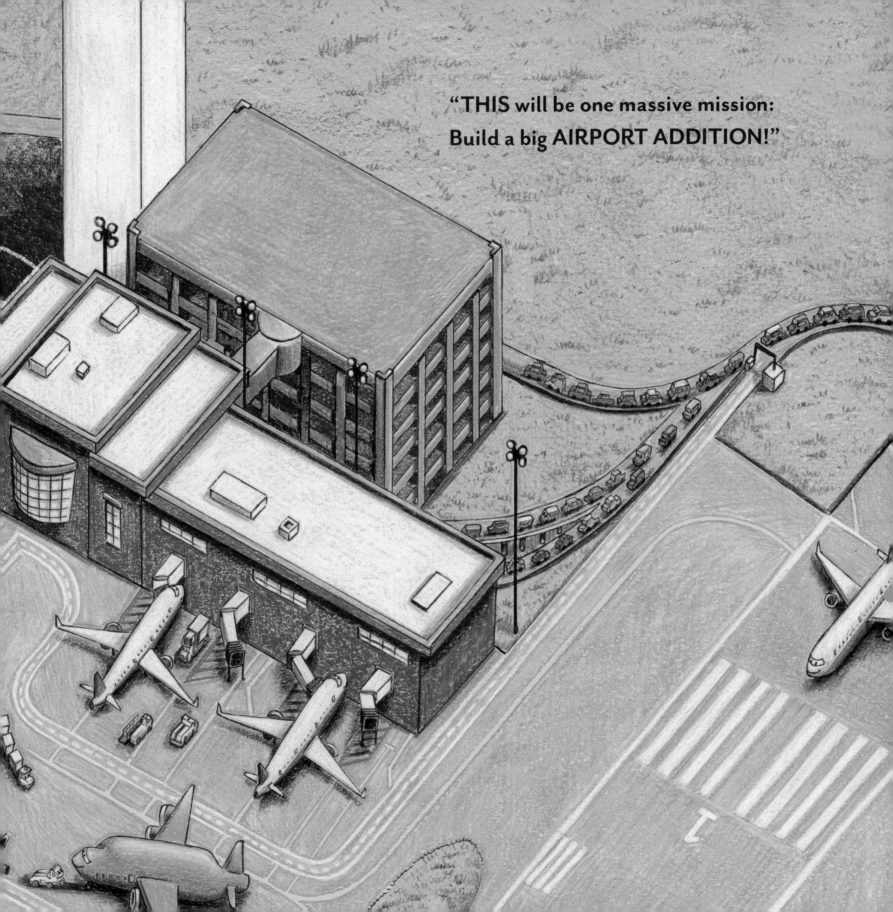

"THIS will be one massive mission:
Build a big AIRPORT ADDITION!"

So many trucks they've never seen
and AWESOME airplanes in between—
they wave hello, and then *they're gone!*
(No one slows or stops for long.)

The airport's an exciting place!
The ground crew keeps a speedy pace;
there's a lot for them to do.

Construction trucks get busy, too!

First Excavator starts to roll.
He digs and scoops to make a hole—
a huge foundation, wide and deep,
and . . . a giant soil heap!

Loader joins the team today,

and Dump Truck hauls the dirt away.

A jet plane flies in from the sky,
touches down, and lands nearby.

She slowly taxis to her marks—
pulls right in, then stops and parks.

Belt Loader pulls up to the side,
and loads of luggage get a ride!
She takes suitcases off the plane.
Then—all aboard the baggage train!

Now here comes Tractor, off to tow
the luggage where it needs to go.

Bulldozer revs and pushes strong
and clears a path *two miles long*!

Cement Mixer pours some fresh concrete—
then it's spread out, all nice and neat.

With more runways for planes to land,
this airport's starting to *expand*.

Hydrant Dispenser fills fuel tanks.
The grateful airplanes all say thanks!

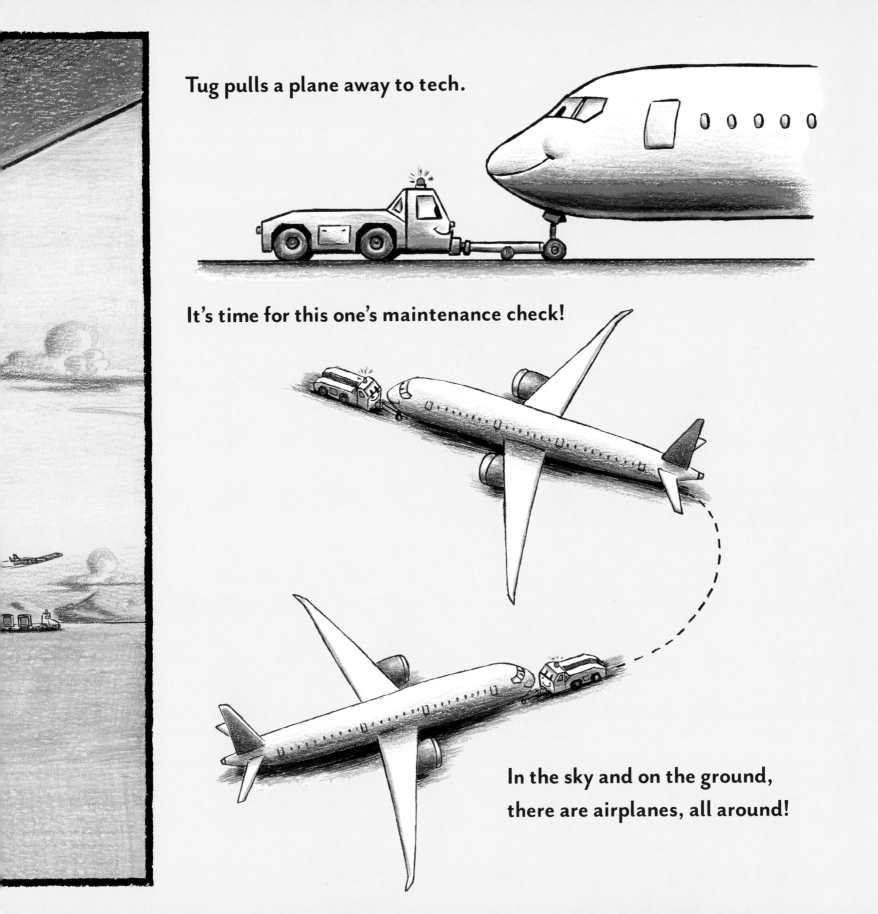

Tug pulls a plane away to tech.

It's time for this one's maintenance check!

In the sky and on the ground,
there are airplanes, all around!

While airplanes wait their turns to fly,
the trucks keep working hard nearby.
When this job is finally done,
no more delays for anyone!

Cargo Plane is taking flight,
hauling TONS with strength and might.

Now Rubber Removal Machine
is getting runways nice and clean:
rolling, spinning, with his scrubber—
erasing airplane tire rubber.
He polishes the landing strip
to help make sure that planes won't slip!

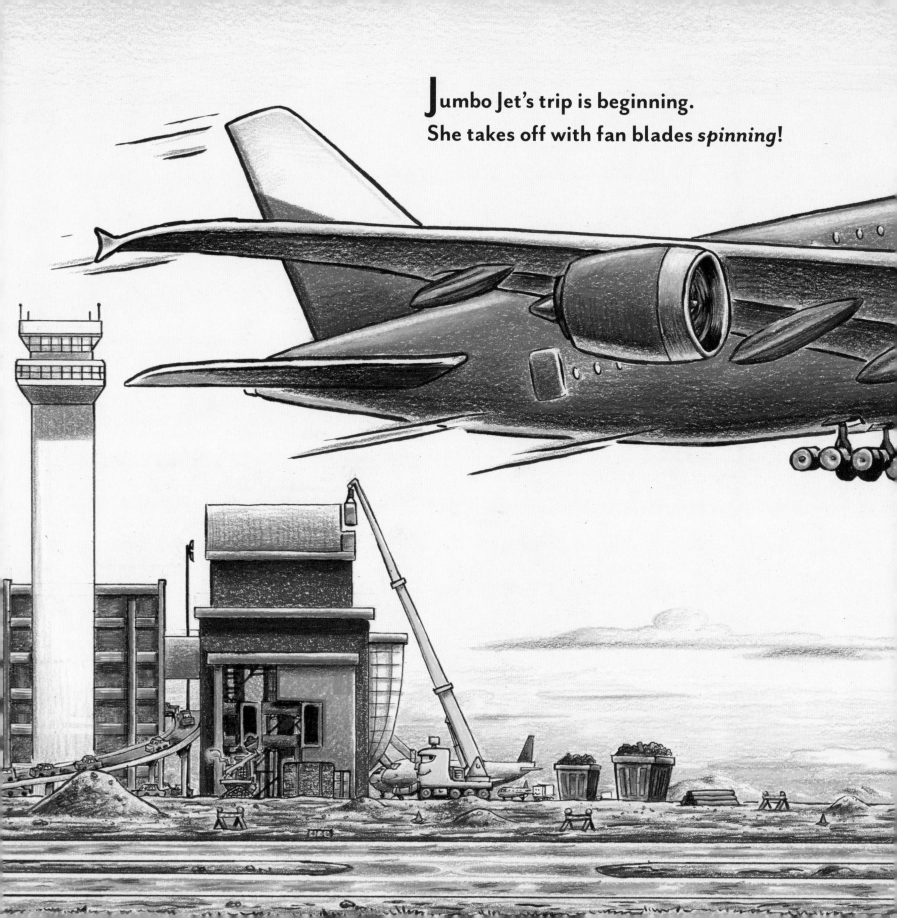

Jumbo Jet's trip is beginning.
She takes off with fan blades *spinning*!

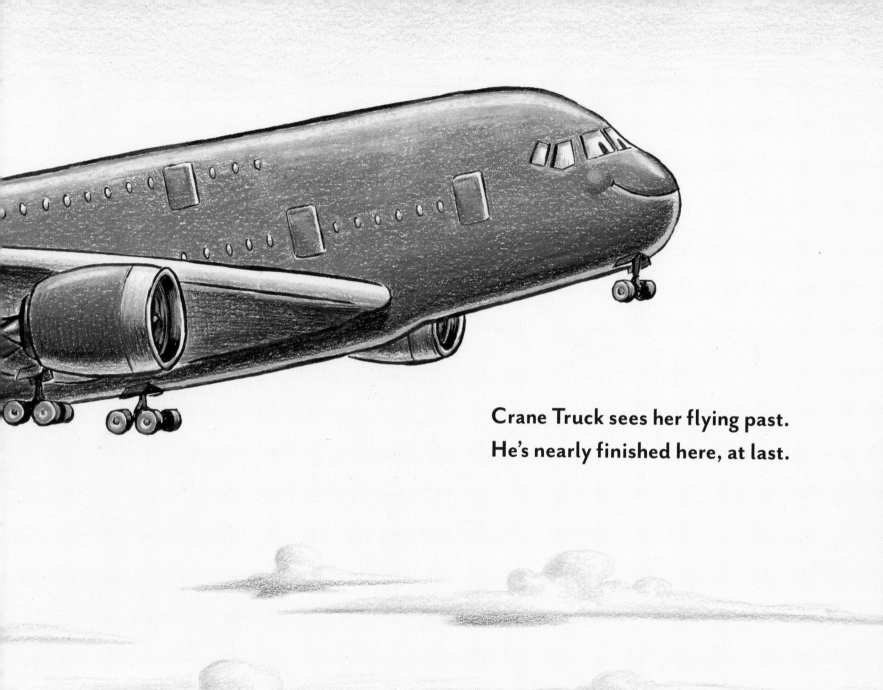

Crane Truck sees her flying past.
He's nearly finished here, at last.

While Crane Truck's lifting loads today,
Lift Truck works, too, not far away.

She drives right in and stops before she lifts *up!* to the airplane door.

Crane Truck sees what she can do.
"I see you like to lift things, too!"

Skid Steer carries heavy stacks.
She rolls on wheels . . .

or on tracks!

With attachments for each chore,
she can lift and push—*and more!*

Her grapple helps her haul a beam.
She works so hard to help the team!

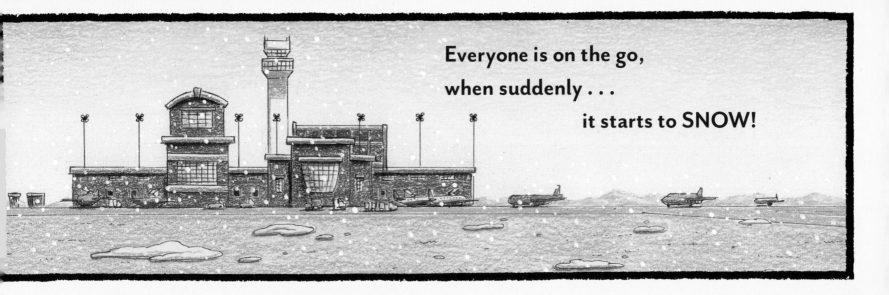

Everyone is on the go,
when suddenly . . .

it starts to SNOW!

An unexpected springtime storm!
Quickly, snowdrifts start to form.

And soon the snow is REALLY HIGH!
The runway's covered! Planes can't fly!

"SNOW-REMOVAL TEAM, let's roll!"

They all line up to take control:
Snowplows gather, then *attack!*
with Sweepers whirling 'round in back.

And here come the mighty Blowers—
awesome, roaring *snowdrift throwers!*

Now Tankers all roll in and spray
some stuff that melts the ice away!

And at last, the runway's clear.
This job is done. The airplanes cheer!

Construction trucks then lend a hand
so ground crew trucks can work as planned.

De-icing Truck now clears the snow
and ice from planes—so they can *go*!
She lifts her boom into the sky—
she aims and sets the pressure high.

With sprayers blasting at full power,
planes get a de-icing shower!
From nose to tail, she sprays each one.
The skies clear as the last plane's done.

This project was a *soaring* feat,
and now this giant job's COMPLETE!

The airport crew all wave goodbye.
"Thanks! Now we can really FLY!"

So another workday ends. . . .
These teams *were* strangers.
                     Now, they're friends.

While plane lights twinkle overhead,
hardworking trucks roll into bed,
drift off to sleep,
and dream of flight.

Good work, big trucks.